RICKY RICOTTA'S
MIGHTY ROBOT
VS. THE JURASSIC JACKRABBITS FROM JUPITER

STORY BY
DAV PILKEY

ART BY
DAN SANTAT

SCHOLASTIC INC.

FOR JOSEPH, GRACE, AND
JACOB RITZERT
– D.P.

FOR MOM AND DAD
– D.S.

Text copyright © 2002, 2014 by Dav Pilkey
www.pilkey.com

Illustrations copyright © 2014 by Dan Santat
www.dantat.com

For information regarding permission, write to Scholastic Inc., Attention:
Permissions Department, 557 Broadway, New York, NY 10012.

Library of Congress Cataloging-in-Publication Data

Pilkey, Dav, 1966 – author.
Ricky Ricotta's mighty robot vs. the Jurassic jackrabbits from Jupiter /
story by Dav Pilkey ; art by Dan Santat. — Revised edition.
pages cm
Summary: General Jackrabbit and his Robo-Rabbits from Jupiter
attempt to take over the world on Ricky Ricotta's birthday.
1. Ricotta, Ricky (Fictitious character) — Juvenile fiction. 2. Mice — Juvenile fiction.
3. Robots — Juvenile fiction. 4. Heroes — Juvenile fiction. 5. Dinosaurs — Juvenile fiction.
6. Jackrabbits — Juvenile fiction. 7. Jupiter (Planet) — Juvenile fiction. [1. Mice — Fiction.
2. Robots — Fiction. 3. Heroes — Fiction. 4. Humorous stories.] I. Santat, Dan, illustrator.
II. Title. III. Title: Ricky Ricotta's mighty robot versus the Jurassic jackrabbits from Jupiter.
PZ7.P63123Rok 2014   813.54 — dc23   2014003714

ISBN 978-0-545-63119-8

10 9 8 7 6 5 4 3   16 17 18 19 20

Printed in China   38

Revised edition
First printing, November 2014

Book design by Phil Falco

CHAPTERS

CHAPTER ONE
BIRTHDAY

One fine morning, Ricky Ricotta
woke up and looked at his calendar.
"It's my birthday!" he shouted.
"Hooray!"

Ricky ran outside in his pajamas and woke up his Mighty Robot.

"It's my birthday! It's my birthday!" shouted Ricky. "This is going to be the *best* day ever!"

First, Ricky's parents cooked
peanut-butter pancakes for breakfast.

Then, Ricky's parents gave him a
present.
"Wow! A new bike!" said Ricky.
"Thank you, Mom and Dad!"

Ricky's Mighty Robot did not have a present for Ricky, but he had an idea.

The Mighty Robot flew high
into the air and spelled out a
birthday message in the sky.

"Thank you, Mighty Robot!"
said Ricky.

Ricky and his Mighty Robot brushed their teeth and got ready to go to the museum.

"We are going to see real dinosaur skeletons today," said Ricky. "This will be the *BEST* day ever!"

"We have one more surprise for you," said Ricky's mother. "Your cousin, Lucy, is coming with us."

"Oh, *NO!*" cried Ricky. "Not Lucy! She is a little *PEST!*"

"She doesn't mean to be a pest," said Ricky's father. "She is just lonely. She has no friends of her own."

"Now, you boys be nice to her," said Ricky's mother.

"*Rats!*" said Ricky. "This is going to be the *WORST* day ever!"

CHAPTER TWO
GENERAL JACKRABBIT

Meanwhile, far off in the solar system (about 560 million miles, to be exact), even *worse* things were happening on a huge orange planet called Jupiter.

Jupiter was the largest planet in the solar system, and it was orange because of all the carrots. You see, Jupiter was the home of billions of carrot-loving jackrabbits.

But sadly, they were all controlled by an evil ruler named General Jackrabbit.

I will not be happy until I take over all the planets in the solar system!" said General Jackrabbit. "And I will start with Earth!"

General Jackrabbit and his
two Robo-Rabbit helpers got
into a rocket ship and blasted
off toward Earth.

CHAPTER THREE
AN EVIL PLAN

The first thing General Jackrabbit saw when he got to Earth was Ricky Ricotta's Mighty Robot.

"Hmmm," said General Jackrabbit. "If I want to take over Earth, I'll have to destroy that Mighty Robot first."

Then he got an evil idea.

General Jackrabbit landed his rocket ship on the roof of the museum . . .

MUSEUM

. . . and he sneaked inside.

TRICERATOPS

TYRANNOSAURUS
REX

CHAPTER FOUR
LUCY THE PEST

Meanwhile, Ricky and his family were getting ready to go to the museum. Lucy had just arrived, and she was already being a pest.

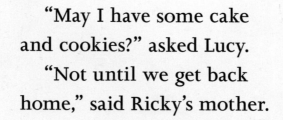

"May I have some cake
and cookies?" asked Lucy.
"Not until we get back
home," said Ricky's mother.

"May I play with the Robot?"
asked Lucy.

"Maybe later," said Ricky's father.

"Will you play princess with me,
Ricky?" asked Lucy.

"No *way!*" said Ricky.

Ricky, Lucy, and Ricky's parents
climbed onto the Mighty Robot's back,
and off they flew to the museum.

"How much longer till we get there?" asked Lucy.

"Soon," said Ricky's father.

"I have to go potty," said Lucy.

"You just went!" said Ricky's mother.

"Can we go ice-skating instead of
going to the museum?" asked Lucy.

"*You* can," said Ricky, smiling. "We'll
drop you off."

Ricky's Mighty Robot giggled.

"*Boys!*" said Ricky's mother. "Be *nice!*"

CHAPTER FIVE
MUSEUM MISHAP

When everyone got to the museum, they noticed that something was not right. The Triceratops looked strange. The Pterodactyl was missing something. And the Tyrannosaurus Rex was all wrong.

TRICERATOPS

TYRANNOSAURUS REX

"The dinosaurs have lost their heads!" cried Lucy.

"Don't worry," said Ricky. "We'll find them!"

Ricky climbed into his Mighty
Robot's hand, and the two friends
flew off to look for the lost dinosaur
heads.

Ricky and his Robot looked all
around the museum. But they did not
think to look on *TOP* of the museum.

CHAPTER SIX
SEND IN THE CLONES

Back on the roof of the museum,
General Jackrabbit was doing
an evil experiment inside his
rocket ship.

He took cells from his three stolen dinosaur skulls and put them into his cloning machine. But the dinosaurs were not complete. General Jackrabbit needed more cells. Where could he get them?

"I know," said General Jackrabbit. "I will add my *own* cells to the dinosaur cells to make them complete!" He clipped some hairs from his fluffy bunny tail and added them to the dinosaur cells. Suddenly, the cloning machine began to work.

In a few minutes, three strange-looking eggs rolled out of the cloning machine.

"Success at last!" shouted General Jackrabbit.

Soon the eggs began to hatch. Out came a Rabbidactyl, a Trihareatops, and a Bunnysaurus Rex.

"Perfect!" said General Jackrabbit.

He carried his Jurassic Jackrabbits up to the nose of his rocket ship and tossed them out. Then he zapped them with his Meany Machiney.

ZAAAAAP!

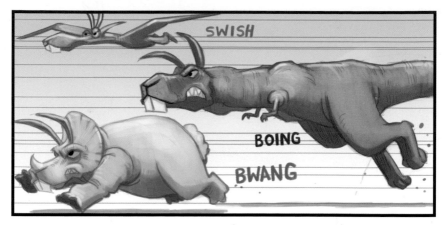

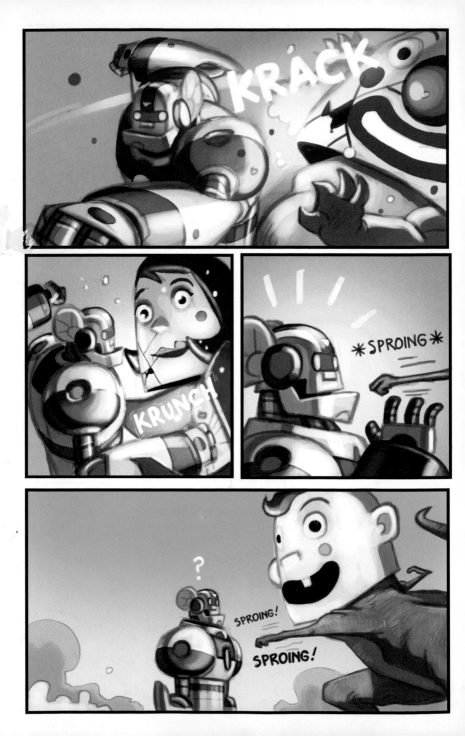

SMASH!

CHAPTER SEVEN
JURASSIC JACK-ATTACK

The three Jurassic Jackrabbits pulled the broken heads off their shoulders. They were very dizzy.

"Don't just sit there," cried General Jackrabbit, "DESTROY THAT MIGHTY ROBOT!!!"

The big, bad bunnies had some terrible
tricks in store for Ricky's Robot. . . .
Like the cotton-tailed creature crasher . . .

. . . and an unpleasant pile of prehistoric power punchies!

But Ricky's Robot had some tricks of his own. First came the electro-reflecto ejector protector.

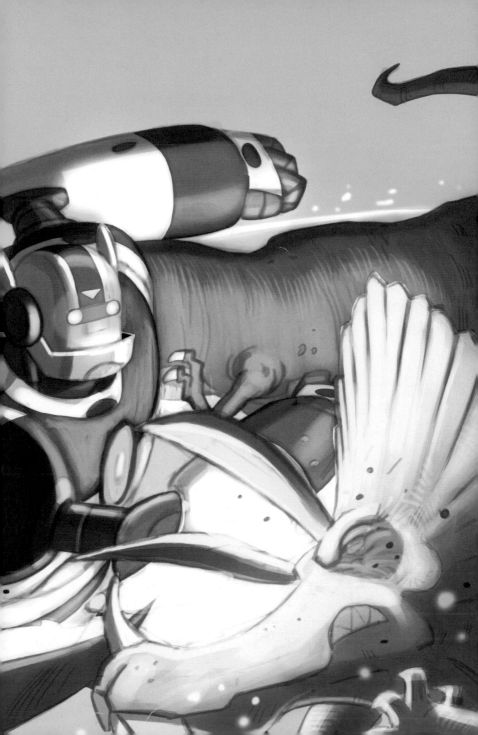

Then came the telescopic
two-ton turbo trasher.

The Jurassic Jackrabbits moaned and groaned.

"Get back out there and fight, you dino-dummies," cried General Jackrabbit, "or I'll give you something to moan and groan about."

CHAPTER EIGHT
THE BIG BATTLE
(IN FLIP-O-RAMA™)

FLIP-O
HEY, KIDS! YOU CAN ANIMATE THE ACTION BY FOLLOWING THESE EASY STEPS!

-RAMA

HERE'S HOW IT WORKS!

STEP 1

Place your *left* hand inside the dotted lines marked "LEFT HAND HERE." Hold the book open *flat*.

STEP 2

Grasp the *right-hand* page with your right thumb and index finger (inside the dotted lines marked "RIGHT THUMB HERE").

STEP 3

Now *quickly* flip the right-hand page back and forth until the picture appears to be *animated*.

(For extra fun, try adding your own sound-effects!)

FLIP-O-RAMA 1

(pages 69 and 71)

Remember, flip *only* page 69.
While you are flipping, be sure you
can see the picture on page 69
and the one on page 71.
If you flip quickly, the two
pictures will start to look like
<u>one</u> *animated* picture.

Don't forget to add
your own sound-effects!

LEFT HAND HERE

THE JURASSIC JACKRABBITS ATTACKED.

RIGHT
THUMB
HERE

RIGHT
INDEX
FINGER
HERE

70

**THE JURASSIC
JACKRABBITS ATTACKED.**

FLIP-O-RAMA 2

(pages 73 and 75)

Remember, flip *only* page 73.
While you are flipping, be sure you
can see the picture on page 73
and the one on page 75.
If you flip quickly, the two
pictures will start to look like
<u>one</u> *animated* picture.

Don't forget to add
your own sound-effects!

LEFT HAND HERE

RICKY'S ROBOT
FOUGHT BACK.

RIGHT
THUMB
HERE

RIGHT
INDEX
FINGER
HERE

74

RICKY'S ROBOT
FOUGHT BACK.

FLIP-O-RAMA 3

(pages 77 and 79)

Remember, flip *only* page 77.
While you are flipping, be sure you
can see the picture on page 77
and the one on page 79.
If you flip quickly, the two
pictures will start to look like
<u>one</u> *animated* picture.

Don't forget to add
your own sound-effects!

LEFT HAND HERE

THE JURASSIC JACKRABBITS BATTLED HARD.

RIGHT
THUMB
HERE

78

THE JURASSIC JACKRABBITS BATTLED HARD.

FLIP-O-RAMA 4

(pages 81 and 83)

Remember, flip only page 81.
While you are flipping, be sure you
can see the picture on page 81
and the one on page 83.
If you flip quickly, the two
pictures will start to look like
one animated picture.

Don't forget to add
your own sound-effects!

LEFT HAND HERE

RICKY'S ROBOT
BATTLED HARDER.

RIGHT
INDEX
FINGER
HERE

82

RICKY'S ROBOT
BATTLED HARDER.

FLIP-O-RAMA 5

(pages 85 and 87)

Remember, flip *only* page 85.
While you are flipping, be sure you
can see the picture on page 85
and the one on page 87.
If you flip quickly, the two
pictures will start to look like
<u>one</u> *animated* picture.

Don't forget to add
your own sound-effects!

LEFT HAND HERE

RICKY'S ROBOT
WON THE WAR.

RIGHT
THUMB
HERE

RIGHT
INDEX
FINGER
HERE

RICKY'S ROBOT
WON THE WAR.

CHAPTER NINE
THE MEANY MACHINEY

The Jurassic Jackrabbits had been
defeated. But General Jackrabbit
was not worried. He just zapped
the Jurassic Jackrabbits with *another*
blast from his Meany Machiney.

The Jurassic Jackrabbits grew even *bigger* than before . . . and much, *much* meaner.

The Jurassic Jackrabbits grabbed Ricky's Mighty Robot in their terrible paws and began laughing and growling.

"I've got to save my Robot!" cried Ricky. He climbed onto the roof of the museum and rang the doorbell on the rocket ship.

Ding-dong.

The two Robo-Rabbits opened the door.

"No mice allowed!" said the Robo-Rabbits. "Jackrabbits ONLY!" Then they slammed the door in Ricky's face.

"Jackrabbits only, eh?" said Ricky. Then he got an idea. "I will need everybody's help today," said Ricky. "Especially Lucy's!"

Ricky's family climbed onto the roof of the museum. Then, Ricky's mother opened her purse. She took out two sticks of gum, a pair of white wool mittens, and an old white scarf.

Quickly, Ricky's family began
dressing up Lucy. The gum made
great bunny teeth . . .

. . . and the scarf made excellent bunny ears. Ricky sewed the mittens together to make a fluffy bunny tail.

"The last thing we need," said Ricky, "is Dad's sweater."

Finally, Lucy climbed onto Ricky's shoulders.

"Now be careful, you two," said Ricky's father.

"Don't worry," said Ricky. "The good guys always win!"

CHAPTER TEN
RICKY AND LUCY TO THE RESCUE

Ricky and Lucy went to the rocket ship and rang the doorbell again. *Ding-dong.*

When the Robo-Rabbits opened the door this time, they saw a beautiful girl rabbit.

"I'm in love," said the first Robo-Rabbit.

"Ooh-la-laaa!" said the second Robo-Rabbit. "Hubba-hubba!" They took Lucy (and Ricky) into the rocket ship and sat them down at a big table.

"I'm hungry!" said Lucy. "May I have some cake and pie and cookies and muffins and cupcakes and bagels and waffles and doughnuts?"

"Yes, yes, yes!" said the Robo-Rabbits, and they ran off to start baking.

"Now is my chance to look around," said Ricky. He crawled out from under the table and sneaked upstairs.

CHAPTER ELEVEN
UPSTAIRS

Upstairs, Ricky saw General Jackrabbit with his horrible Meany Machiney.

"Now, Jurassic Jackrabbits, I want you to destroy that Mighty Ro—" General Jackrabbit stopped suddenly and sniffed the air.

Sniff, sniff, sniff.

"Hey!" shouted General Jackrabbit.
"Somebody's baking *carrot pie*!
What are those silly Robo-Rabbits
up to now?"

General Jackrabbit marched downstairs to see what the problem was. As soon as he was gone, Ricky ran to the Meany Machiney and studied the complex controls.

Ricky turned the dial from BIG, UGLY, 'N' EVIL all the way over to LITTLE, CUTE, 'N' SWEET. Then he pointed the Meany Machiney at the Jurassic Jackrabbits.

BIG, UGLY, 'N' EVIL

MEDIUM-SIZED AVERAGE-LOOKING 'N' ETHICALLY NEUTRA

LITTLE, CUTE, 'N' SWEET

CHAPTER TWELVE
ZAP!

Downstairs, General Jackrabbit was yelling at his Robo-Rabbits when he heard a loud *ZAP!*

"What's going on up there?" he cried.

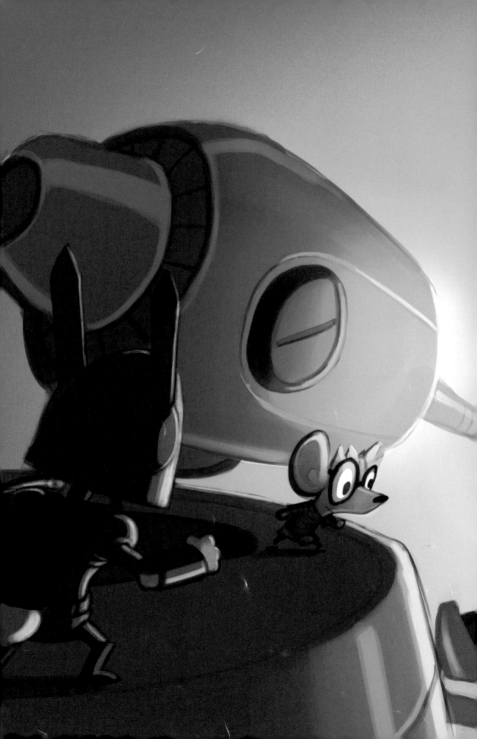

General Jackrabbit dashed upstairs.
He saw Ricky zapping the Jurassic
Jackrabbits. The three creatures got
littler, cuter, and sweeter with each zap.

"I'LL GET YOU FOR THIS!" screamed General Jackrabbit. He grabbed Ricky by the arm and would not let go.

Suddenly, Lucy appeared at the top of the stairs with a fresh carrot pie.

"Yoo-hoo!" sang Lucy.

General Jackrabbit turned around and . . .

. . . SPLAT!!!

CHAPTER THIRTEEN
THE DAY IS SAVED

Ricky's Mighty Robot jumped up to the rocket ship to rescue Ricky and Lucy.

"Now we've got to make things right again," said Ricky.

First, Ricky's Robot put the
dinosaur skulls back where they
belonged . . . sort of.

Then, Ricky's Robot carefully closed the rocket ship. With one mighty toss, the Robot sent the ship sailing safely back to Jupiter.

"Bye-bye, Robo-Rabbits!" cried Lucy.

Finally, it was off to jail for
General Jackrabbit.
"*This has been the worst day
ever!*" cried General Jackrabbit.

CHAPTER FOURTEEN
FRIENDS

Soon Ricky and his family got
home. It was time for pizza and
birthday cake.

"I sure love these cute little Jurassic Jackrabbits," said Lucy.

"Then you should keep them," said Ricky. "Now you'll have little friends of your own!"

"Really?" asked Lucy. "Are you sure you don't want them?"

"I don't need them," said Ricky.
"I already have the biggest friend
in town!"

Finally, Ricky blew out the candles on his cake.

"You know," said Ricky, "this really was the best day ever!"

"Thank you for being so brave today," said Ricky's parents.

"And thank you for sharing," said Lucy.

"No problem," said Ricky . . .

. . . "that's what friends are for!"

READY FOR

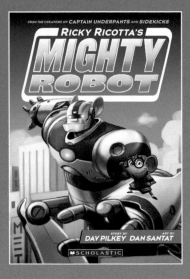

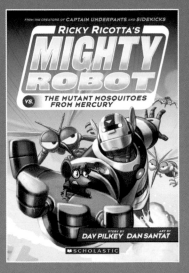

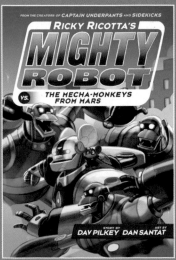

MORE RICKY?

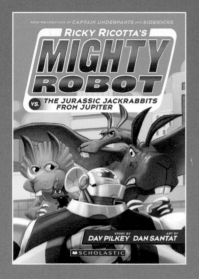

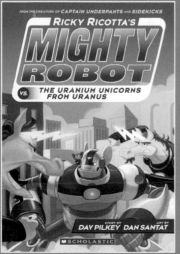

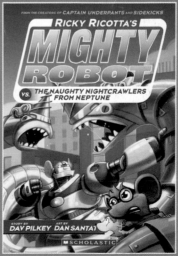

DAV PILKEY

has written and illustrated more than fifty books for children, including *The Paperboy*, a Caldecott Honor book; *Dog Breath: The Horrible Trouble with Hally Tosis*, winner of the California Young Reader Medal; and the IRA Children's Choice Dumb Bunnies series. He is also the creator of the *New York Times* bestselling Captain Underpants books. Dav lives in the Pacific Northwest with his wife. Find him online at www.pilkey.com.

DAN SANTAT

is the writer and illustrator of the picture book *The Adventures of Beekle: The Unimaginary Friend*. He is also the creator of the graphic novel *Sidekicks* and has illustrated many acclaimed picture books, including the *New York Times* bestseller *Because I'm Your Dad* by Ahmet Zappa and *Crankenstein* by Samantha Berger. Dan also created the Disney animated hit *The Replacements*. He lives in Southern California with his family. Find him online at www.dantat.com.